Play
The Plague Trilogy
Book II

MARILYN KAYE

BANTAM BOOKS
NEW YORK • TORONTO • LONDON • SYDNEY • AUCKLAND

For Jane Furse,
who knows many good jokes
and shares them with me

RL 5.5, 008–012
PLAY
A Bantam Skylark Book / June 2002

ISBN 0-553-48764-7

Visit us on the Web! www.randomhouse.com/kids

Published simultaneously in the United States and Canada

Bantam Skylark is an imprint of Random House Children's Books, a division of
Random House, Inc. SKYLARK BOOK and colophon and BANTAM BOOKS
and colophon are registered trademarks of Random House, Inc. Bantam Books,
1540 Broadway, New York, New York 10036.

PRINTED IN THE UNITED STATES OF AMERICA

OPM   10   9   8   7   6   5   4   3   2   1

Play

one

Looking around, Amy Candler could see that the hospital waiting room hadn't changed. The same metal folding chairs lined the wall, facing signs that directed people to emergency exits, advised them to speak softly, and ordered them not to smoke. The same pungent smells of antiseptic and medicine permeated the air. Everything was still sterile white. And the same hollow voice paged doctors from an invisible intercom.

It was all depressingly familiar. The French phrase *déjà vu,* "already seen," came to Amy. But for Amy, this wasn't just *déjà vu.* She *had* been here, just two weeks ago. She might even have been sitting in this very same folding chair, waiting for a report on her mother's condition.

Nancy Candler was fine now. In fact, she was sitting next to Amy in the waiting room, along with Eric Morgan and his parents. This time, they were all anxious for a report on Tasha's health.

"We can't stop hoping," Mrs. Morgan said as she tried to comfort her husband. His face was buried in his hands. "Tasha could make a complete recovery. People *do* recover. Look at Nancy. She's perfectly healthy now."

Amy hoped those thoughts gave Tasha's father some encouragement. To her own ears, Mrs. Morgan's words were feeble and unconvincing. Eric, Tasha's brother, didn't seem bolstered by them either. He was staring dismally into space. No doubt that was because he knew the real reason why Nancy Candler had recovered so completely and so quickly.

Abruptly, Eric got up and walked down the hall to the water fountain. Amy rose and followed him. She knew him well enough to see that he was trying not to cry. So she waited while he took long, thirsty gulps of water—no doubt a ruse to hide the fact that he was upset. By the time he turned to face Amy, his face was stony again.

He waited while Amy took a sip of water and then asked, "Can't you do it again?" The question came out of the blue, but she knew what he was talking about. He wanted to know why she couldn't save Tasha the way she had saved her mother.

Only two weeks ago, Amy had gone millions of years back in time on a mission to find the source of the Plague. She'd returned to the present with a blood-stain that had provided an antidote—but only enough for one dose. Her dying mother was cured, but the Plague raged on. Eric was hoping Amy could go back to the Stone Age and return with another dose of antidote for Tasha.

"I tried," Amy told him. "I went back to that think tank, Singularity, this morning. But they can't send me back in time again."

"Why?"

"Because they're gone."

"What do you mean they're gone?"

"I mean they've vanished, Eric. The office is occupied by a podiatrist. I went in and asked about Singularity, but no one knew where the think tank had moved to. I even called Information, but there was no listing."

"What about the people who worked there?"

"We never knew Sarah's and Howard's last names," Amy replied.

"What about Devon?"

"Oh, Eric, don't you think I've tried to contact him?

But it's impossible. He turns up only when he wants to." The mysterious Mr. Devon had been popping up in Amy's life for two years now, usually when she was involved in a crisis. She was definitely in a crisis now, but so far, there'd been no sign of him. "Besides, even if I could travel back in time again, there's no guarantee I could obtain more blood. What happened before was an accident."

"But there must be something you can do!" Eric cried out angrily. "You've got powers! You can't let Tasha die!" His eyes were tearing up again.

So were Amy's. "Eric, if there was something I could do, I would do it! You know I'd do anything to save Tasha!"

Eric wiped his eyes. "Yeah, I know. I'm sorry, I shouldn't have yelled at you."

"That's okay," Amy said. "I understand." For the past fourteen years, Eric had teased and tormented his kid sister relentlessly. But there was never any doubt that he loved her dearly. As did Amy.

Tasha and Amy had been best friends as long as Amy could remember. Living next door to each other in a West Los Angeles garden-apartment condo, they'd been hanging together since kindergarten. They were as close as sisters. In fact, Tasha, along with her brother, had been in on Amy's big secret from the beginning, when Amy herself had learned of her special nature.

They knew she was a genetically engineered clone, one of thirteen girls who had been created in a laboratory through an experiment known as Project Crescent. They knew that her mother, Nancy Candler, wasn't her birth parent but a scientist who had rescued the seventh clone from a fire in the laboratory and raised the infant as her own. The laboratory had been destroyed by the scientists themselves once they'd learned that their project was sponsored by a top-secret government organization intent on creating a master race to rule the world.

Tasha and Eric knew that Amy's genetic enhancements gave her special powers. Physically and mentally, she was superior to normal teens. Among her friends, only Tasha and Eric knew this, and they'd kept her secret—not only to keep the curious away, but to protect her from the organization. That group knew the clones had survived the laboratory fire, and had never ceased attempting to reach its goal. The organization had been personally involved in several of Amy's confrontations with danger.

Amy's relationship with Eric had been through

many phases. When she was younger, Eric had ignored her the same way he ignored his sister. When Amy was twelve and he was fourteen, they'd become friends, then more than friends. A year ago, that more-than-friends relationship had dissolved, and for a while they had barely spoken. Now they were just friends again.

But through it all, Amy's friendship with Tasha had remained constant. Sure, they'd had their share of ups and downs—arguments, hurt feelings, even moments of real anger—but those times never lasted too long. Amy knew that she and Tasha shared the special bond of being best friends. So the thought of losing Tasha was too horrible for Amy to contemplate. But the Plague had already claimed numerous lives worldwide, and when it didn't kill, it often caused its victims horrible physical damage.

Amy and Eric were still standing by the water fountain. The Morgans and Amy's mother remained in their chairs. They were all silent—in fact, near-silence pervaded this place. Even the passing hospital workers made very little noise, speaking in hushed tones.

The quiet made the ringing of a cell phone sound more shrill than usual. It wasn't until several nurses shot reproving looks at Amy that she realized the noise was coming from her bag.

She dived into her purse and extracted the phone. "Hello?" she said softly.

"Amy, it's Chris."

"Oh. Hi."

Chris, a former classmate (and another more-than-friend), had left Los Angeles with Andy, one of Amy's male clone counterparts. They were on a mission to discover what the organization was currently up to.

"I've got some news," Chris said.

Under normal circumstances, Amy would have been very interested. But her fears for Tasha far outweighed any curiosity she had about the organization. "Chris, I can't talk now," she said. "I'm at Northside Hospital."

"Your mother again?"

"No. Tasha."

Chris uttered a word that would have sent him straight to detention if he had been back at Parkside Middle School. But at the moment the word seemed entirely appropriate.

"Yeah," Amy agreed. "It's bad, Chris. Look, I have to—"

He broke in. "I'm here in Los Angeles, and I need to see you. Right away."

"Chris, I can't leave when—"

He interrupted again. "What I've got to tell you might help Tasha. Meet me at the hospital coffee shop in half an hour." He hung up.

Eric was looking at her with a faint glimmer of curiosity. Amy related Chris's side of the conversation. "I don't know what he's talking about," she told Eric. "The last I heard, he and Andy were on the East Coast, trying to locate some secret organization lab where more clones were being created."

"But he said he's got information that could help Tasha?"

Amy nodded and glanced at her watch. "He wants me to meet him in the coffee shop here in thirty minutes."

"I'm going with you," Eric said.

Amy didn't object. But she hoped Eric wasn't getting his hopes up too high. Whatever news Chris had, she seriously doubted it would provide Tasha with a cure.

They went back to join their parents. Sitting in silence, Amy tried to imagine what Chris and Andy could possibly have learned. She didn't know how it could be relevant to Tasha. As evil as the organization was, the group didn't have anything to do with the Plague. They couldn't be held responsible for it.

Doctors and scientists had been studying the mysterious disease since its first appearance months ago. All they had come up with was the fact that it had a genetic origin. But unlike common genetic disorders passed from generation to generation, this one seemed to pop up out of nowhere.

It was Amy who had discovered its origin. During her journey back in time, she'd learned that an advanced alien contingent from another planet had wanted to colonize Earth during the Stone Age. They hadn't succeeded—but they'd left behind a terrible souvenir of their visit. Bacteria common to their species had damaged a human gene. The gene had lain dormant for millions of years until it had suddenly become active.

Now that deadly gene was alive and wreaking havoc in Tasha's body. And even though Amy doubted Chris could shed any light on it, she couldn't take her eyes off her watch as the next thirty minutes slowly passed.

Chris Skinner was waiting for them in the coffee shop when they walked in. It had been more than a month since Amy had last seen him. His hair was longer, his leather jacket a little more battered, but otherwise he looked the same. He was alone at a small, square table. Eric didn't even go through the usual greetings.

"What do you know?" he asked bluntly.

"Lots," Chris said. "Have a seat and keep your voice low."

"Where's Andy?" Amy asked as they sat down.

"He's still at the lab in Maryland."

"What lab?" Eric asked.

"That's what I came to tell you about." Chris turned to Amy. "Andy told me how you went back to the Stone Age. That must have been pretty amazing."

"It was," Amy confirmed. "There were dinosaurs, you know. Scientists say they died out before the Stone Age, but—"

Eric broke in. "Hey, could we skip the natural history, please? My sister could be dying. I really don't want to hear about dinos right now."

Amy understood his lack of patience. "Tasha's in bad shape, Chris. Have you learned anything about the Plague?"

"Not exactly," Chris said. "But we found out something very interesting about what the organization has been doing lately."

Before Chris could continue, Eric pushed back his chair, making a loud, angry scraping sound. "Look, Skinner, if you don't know anything that can help Tasha, I'm not sticking around here while she's dying three flights up."

Amy spoke calmly. "Eric, sit down and listen. You can't help Tasha by going back to the waiting room. Let's hear what Chris has to say."

Eric ran his fingers through his hair. "Sorry," he muttered. "I'm kind of upset."

"I understand," Chris said. "But what we learned about the organization could lead us to a cure for the Plague."

Eric sat back down. "Okay. I'm listening."

"This is all going to sound pretty weird," Chris warned them. "But I swear, it's happening. Now, you know what the organization's goal is, right?"

"To create a master race," Amy replied automatically. "Of course I know the goal. That's why Andy and I and all the other Andys and Amys were created with our refined genetic structure. Ultimately, we're all supposed to mate and produce superior people who can take over the world. What else is new?"

"It seems that they're exploring more ways of accomplishing their goal," Chris reported. "You clones have given them so much trouble, they're looking at other options."

This *was* news to Amy. "Like what?"

"We found out about a lab they've taken over. At first we thought we were on to another clone factory, but it's nothing like that. They're doing some cutting-edge genetics work, Amy. Something completely new. It's a way of getting into the human body, of eliminating the genes that limit human potential and pumping up the genes that can make people stronger and healthier and help them live longer. It's a way of creating a master race from existing people, without having to wait until genetically engineered clones grow up."

Amy considered this interesting information. "Are you saying they're messing around with the DNA code?"

"No."

"Then are they extracting genes and replacing them?"

"No. Like I said, it's all being done from *inside* the body."

"How?" Eric asked.

"This is where it gets really weird." Chris gazed at them both intensely. "They're injecting a miniature human into the body."

There was a moment of silence as Amy and Eric absorbed this. Eric was the first to respond. "Oh, give me a break," he groaned. "Is that what you and Andy think? You've gotta be kidding."

That was Amy's initial reaction too. But Chris shook his head. "It's not what we think, it's what we *know*. It's all there, in the laboratory. They've actually got some sort of radioactive phototechnology that can reduce a human being to the size of a gene. It allows them to inject a human into a cell nucleus."

"What do you mean?" Amy asked.

"Andy and I hacked into their computer files and got the report on the first attempt. Here's a printout." Chris dug into his backpack and pulled out some papers.

Amy bent over the printout, and Eric looked over her shoulder. There were a lot of technical jargon and data symbols that meant nothing to her. But she was able to interpret enough to realize that this new procedure wasn't a figment of Chris's imagination. And according to this report, the process had worked.

A human, identified only as X, had been reduced by the new technology to the microscopic size of a gene. He was injected into a cell nucleus of someone identified as the Subject, with instructions as to how he should locate the particular gene that caused the Subject to be color-blind.

But there had been problems. X was able to attach himself to the appropriate gene, and both he and the gene were extracted from the Subject's genome. The gene that caused color-blindness was altered and reintroduced. The Subject was cured of his visual disability.

However, during the natural efforts by the Subject's body to reject the intruder X, the genetic structure of X was severely damaged. X survived the process and was brought back to his normal size—but his genes took such a beating that he was permanently altered. The report didn't specify what damage he had suffered, but it must have been dramatic. According to the final section of the report, it was recommended that further experimentation be postponed until some means of protecting the "integrity of the reduced entity" could be developed.

"What do you think happened to him?" Eric asked. "X, I mean."

Amy didn't even want to guess. X could have lost his own vision. He might be unable to walk. He could even be in a vegetative state. Anything was possible. She wondered how the organization had convinced someone to put himself in that position. Of course, given the nature of the organization, they probably hadn't asked for volunteers. They might be scientists and doctors, but they were not moral or ethical. Some poor guy must have been forced to act as the pioneer.

"They have to be stopped," Amy declared. "This isn't right."

Chris shrugged. "Genetic alteration is a big deal right now. Medical science is constantly looking for means of changing the genetic makeup of a human."

"Sure, to cure a person of a genetic disorder," Amy said. "Not to create superior people. It's wrong. And they can't be allowed to put other lives in danger. That's got to be illegal."

"I don't think the organization cares much about what's right or wrong," Chris noted. "Or illegal."

Eric was still looking at the report. "Geez, this sounds like it could really work. I mean, it makes sense, y'know?"

"They've got a lot of kinks to work out first," Amy reminded him. "But hopefully, they won't have the opportunity to do that." She looked at Chris. "Have you and Andy turned this report over to authorities? Like the FBI?"

"No," Chris said. "Not yet."

"Why not?" Amy demanded. "This is just the kind of evidence that could put the organization out of business."

"But it could also lead the government to you and the other Project Crescent clones," Chris said. "Andy thinks we'd better keep this to ourselves for now."

Reluctantly, Amy had to admit that Andy was right. Unless Amy and Andy and all the other clones were willing to subject themselves to worldwide attention, the organization's evil plans would proceed.

"It's too bad," she said. "If this technology was in the hands of reputable people, they could work on replacing the human with some sort of device that could be injected into the genes instead."

"Or figure out how to make it safe for a human to be reduced and get into a body," Chris said.

Eric had been silent for a while. He was still studying the report. Now he looked up and spoke. "This could cure the Plague."

"In theory," Amy said again.

"But isn't that how every great discovery begins?" Eric asked. "With a theory?"

"Sure, but it could take years and years for the theory to become practical," Amy pointed out.

Eric's expression hardened. "My sister doesn't have years to wait for a cure."

Amy gazed at him. "What are you thinking, Eric? Would you really offer Tasha to the organization as a subject for an experiment? You want them to reduce another human victim and inject that person into her body?"

"I'd do anything to save Tasha's life," Eric declared.

"Even at the risk of taking another person's life?"

Eric hesitated. "Maybe it wouldn't have to be a big risk. Like . . . if the person who was injected was . . . you know . . . special."

"Special how?" Chris asked.

"Well . . . like, maybe not so easily damaged."

"Eric, you're not making any sense," Amy said. "No one could survive this procedure without injury. Being reduced, injected into a cell, messing around in a chromosome with a bunch of genes—who could emerge from something like that and still be normal?"

"Maybe someone with a superior genetic structure," Eric replied.

Amy gasped as the impact of what he was saying hit her.

Chris, too, was staring at Eric in disbelief. "Are you talking about *Amy*?" he asked.

"You're Tasha's best friend!" Eric pleaded. "Wouldn't you do this for her?"

Amy was momentarily at a loss for words. When she found them, they poured out in a rush. "Eric, are you crazy? You're asking me to turn myself over to the organization! Can you imagine what they might do to me?"

Chris agreed. "This can't happen, Eric. It's way too dangerous. But Andy and I were thinking that Amy could show this report to her mother's friend Dr. Hopkins. He could use it for his own research on the Plague. Maybe it'll lead him to a cure."

Eric slumped in his seat. "But not in time to save Tasha."

There was silence at the table. Chris looked at the clock on the wall. "I gotta go. There's a guy with a private plane who promised me a lift back east. I'll call you if we get any new leads."

"Okay," Amy said. "Say hi to Andy for me. And be careful."

She sat quietly with Eric for another moment. She could feel his despair, and she shared it. But she wasn't about to give up hope.

"Come on, let's go upstairs," she said. "Maybe there's some good news."

three
3

When they returned to the waiting room, Dr. Dave Hopkins was talking to Tasha's anxious parents. It was clear from their sober expressions that he wasn't giving them good news. Dr. Dave greeted Amy and Eric with a warm smile, but not a happy one.

"Tasha's not suffering," he assured them. "But she's fallen into a coma."

"When will she wake up?" Eric asked. Dr. Dave didn't respond immediately, so Eric rephrased the question. "*Will* she wake up?"

"I don't know," the doctor replied. "I wish I could be more optimistic. Or more specific. We know so little about the Plague. Believe me, we're doing everything we can."

A sob escaped Mrs. Morgan's lips. Nancy Candler took her hand, and Tasha's mother tried to smile through her tears.

"Her vital signs are stable," Dr. Dave continued. "We'll reevaluate her condition in twelve hours. Meanwhile, I suggest that you all go home and get some rest."

But the Morgans wouldn't budge. Amy's mother stood up. "I'm going to take Amy home and feed her."

"Mom!"

Nancy ignored her. "We'll come back with dinner for the Morgans. Come on, Amy."

Her voice carried that "don't argue with me" tone that Amy knew all too well. Promising Eric she'd be back soon, Amy headed out. As she and her mother were leaving, a page came over the intercom.

"Dr. Hopkins, Dr. David Hopkins, extension 234."

Looking over her shoulder, Amy saw Dr. Dave moving toward the nurses' station. She frowned. "He shouldn't leave Tasha."

"He has other patients," Nancy reminded her gently.

Amy didn't care about other patients. Right now, no one in the world mattered to her except Tasha.

At least her mother knew better than to try to cheer her up on the way home. She left Amy alone with her thoughts as they drove.

"Why don't you go upstairs and lie down for a while?" was her only suggestion when they arrived at their condo. "I'll fix a sandwich and bring it up to you."

"I'm not hungry," Amy said, even though she knew Nancy would ignore that comment—just as Amy would ignore the suggestion to lie down. Once Amy was in her room, she sat down at her desk and tried to think.

For the zillionth time in the past few days, she tried all the phone numbers associated with Mr. Devon that she'd collected over the years. But with each effort, she got the same recording: "The number you have dialed is no longer in service."

She turned on her computer and tried old e-mail addresses for the mysterious man, but none was operating. Searches turned up nothing.

Frustrated, she thought back to her earlier conversation with Chris. If the organization really had a means of attacking the Plague . . . and if Chris or Andy knew how she could contact the organization . . . but she pushed that notion out of her head. The organization was evil. She knew that for a fact. They had no reason in the world to save Tasha. And once they'd reduced Amy to the size of a gene . . . Amy shuddered. The organization would have complete control over her.

It wasn't just for her personal safety that Amy rejected the idea. Given the goals of the organization, she had the whole world to protect. There was no way she'd voluntarily offer herself up to that group. It wouldn't save Tasha, and it could put humanity at risk. She'd end up being a martyr for no good reason.

She clenched her fists and closed her eyes. There had to be something she hadn't thought of yet. Just then she heard the doorbell ring downstairs, but she ignored it. She wasn't expecting anyone, and her mother would send whoever it was away.

So she was surprised a few minutes later when she heard her mother call out, "Amy, come down here." Surely her mother knew she wasn't interested in any company. But she got up anyway.

Dr. Dave was in the living room with her mother. And they weren't alone.

"Mr. Devon!"

Even as she gaped at the mysterious man, Amy realized she shouldn't be so surprised to see him. After all, it was his habit to show up when least expected—and most needed.

"Hi," she said. It seemed like an inadequate greeting,

but she couldn't think of anything else to say. Devon acknowledged her with a brief nod before turning to Nancy.

"You have completely recovered?" he asked.

"Yes," Nancy replied. She seemed slightly dazed.

Dr. Dave was looking at Devon with awe and respect. "Mr. Devon told us how you brought the blood back from the Stone Age," he said to Amy. As he spoke, he was shaking his head, as if he still hadn't completely absorbed the information.

"Then it's true?" Amy mother asked. "You . . . you went back in time?"

Amy nodded.

"And you saved my life." Nancy gazed at her daughter in wonderment.

Amy nodded again. "And I want to do it again, if I can save Tasha."

"There is a better way," Mr. Devon said. "If you are willing, you may be able to save not only Tasha, but everyone afflicted with the Plague."

Amy's heartbeat quickened. She'd known Mr. Devon would have a plan! "That's wonderful!" she shouted. "I'll do it!"

"Wait a minute," Dr. Dave said. "What does this 'better way' involve?"

"Is it dangerous?" Nancy asked.

"It involves less risk to the human body than time travel," Devon replied. "With Amy's superior genetic condition, there will be no danger at all."

Her mother looked relieved, but Amy gazed at Mr. Devon curiously. That wasn't the kind of thing he usually said. Normally, he didn't dismiss the possibility of danger so quickly. If anything, he reprimanded Amy for not being sufficiently cautious.

"Can you be more specific?" Dr. Dave asked Devon.

"Yes, of course. There is a new technology that combines dehydration, particle transfiguration, and centrifugal force in a vacuum cabinet. Through this mechanism, a person can be reduced to the size of a gene and injected into a cell nucleus. By searching through chromosomes, this person could discover the Plague gene. The Plague gene and the person gene would then be withdrawn from the diseased body, and the person would be . . ." He seemed to be searching for a word. ". . . reconstituted. Brought back to his or her natural size."

Dr. Dave was frowning. "Are you saying that a human has to be reduced and injected into each person who suffers from the Plague?"

"Not at all," Mr. Devon said. "From the analysis of one Plague gene, a chemical antidote that can destroy all Plague genes will be created. We need only for someone to bring out that one Plague gene."

Amy's mother was appalled. "And you want to use Amy to get that gene out? I don't think so."

Amy didn't put up an argument. She, too, was looking at Mr. Devon with horror. "I've heard about this procedure. The organization came up with the technology!"

Mr. Devon turned to her with a blank expression. "I beg your pardon?"

"It's how they're going to make superior people—by fiddling with their genes from the inside!"

"I have no knowledge of this," Mr. Devon said. "I am simply presenting a technology that could save people who are currently afflicted with a terrible disease." He turned to Dr. Dave. "For an ordinary person, the reduction process could be dangerous. But for someone like Amy, there should be no health risk."

Dr. Dave nodded slowly and turned to Nancy. "He's right, you know. With close monitoring, Amy should have no problem surviving a procedure like this."

"And she *will* be monitored," Mr. Devon assured them. "She will be tracked throughout her journey. At any sign of danger to her, she can be immediately extracted."

Amy looked at her mother. "I don't know," Nancy said. "I just don't know." For once, Amy didn't try to talk her mother into giving permission. Something about this whole conversation was making her extremely uneasy. It wasn't just the subject matter. It was Mr. Devon. Amy tried to remember if he'd always spoken so stiffly, without expression, without using any contractions.

She stepped back to get a broader perspective and looked him over carefully. How could she even be sure he was the real Mr. Devon—and not a Devon clone?

On the island where the genetically designed Project Crescent clones had been gathered for testing last summer, Amy had discovered the existence of Devon clones. Some had been aligned with the organization. Others—at least, one other—had helped the Amys and Andys escape. She conjured up an image of that particular Devon, with a remote control in his hand, sending their boat away from the island and the kidnappers. She'd assumed that he was the original Devon, the one who'd helped her many times. When she had encountered him upon her return from the Stone Age, she hadn't even questioned him—she'd had no doubts that he was the good guy, and he'd proved it by saving her mother.

But this time . . . how could she be sure? How did she know he hadn't been sent by the organization to lure her into their hands? Maybe there were some questions she could ask him. His ability—or inability—to answer correctly might reveal his true identity.

As she contemplated the many experiences she'd had with the one real Mr. Devon, she became aware that Devon, Dr. Dave, and her mother had continued to speak together in low tones. Now her mother was gazing at her worriedly.

"Amy . . ."

"It's okay, Mom," Amy said quickly, thinking her mother would be relieved that Amy wasn't going to beg and plead.

"You're not frightened?" her mother asked. "You're willing to do this to save Tasha?"

"Not to mention the rest of the world," Dr. Dave added.

Amy's eyes widened. Were they about to agree to Devon's plan?

But why wouldn't they? Dr. Dave knew how Devon had saved Nancy. And Nancy had always trusted Devon. Two years ago, when Amy discovered the truth about herself, Mr. Devon had posed as the assistant principal of her school. He'd protected Amy and been supportive of Nancy. Why wouldn't she believe him now?

Dr. Dave was looking at her with admiration. "You're a brave girl, Amy."

"You amaze me," her mother said simply. "I've always

loved you, sweetie, but now I'm in awe of you. You saved my life, you'll save Tasha's life, and you'll save the world."

"Yes," Mr. Devon said. "She is a fine person. She will be making a great contribution to society."

For a second, Amy couldn't breathe. Nor could she completely grasp the notion that somehow this man—who quite possibly was an emissary of her worst enemy—had convinced two rational adults and brilliant scientists that she should take on this mission. Now Dr. David Hopkins and her very own mother were looking at her with love, respect, and admiration for her dedication and courage.

How could she possibly tell them that she was more frightened than she'd ever been in her life?

four

"**O**f course, we cannot assume that the genes will immediately accept your presence," Mr. Devon said as they sat around the table in a laboratory at the hospital. "It is the natural response of the human body to reject any unknown element. But hopefully, it will recognize Amy as a friend, not an intruder."

"How am I supposed to let it know I'm a friend?" Amy asked. "Do I have to wave a white handkerchief?"

"Amy, this is no time to joke around," her mother chided her.

As far as Amy was concerned, this was exactly the time to joke around. It was the only way she could hide her fear. She still couldn't believe this was happening. She couldn't believe that her mother was going along with such a far-fetched plan. This was a woman who freaked out if she couldn't reach Amy on her cell phone. Just last week, she'd refused Amy permission to hang with some friends at a downtown coffee shop. So how could she let her daughter wander off into a human cell?

But clearly, her mother believed Amy would be safer in Tasha's body than she would be in downtown L.A. "We'll be able to track her at all times, won't we?" she was asking Mr. Devon.

"Yes, she will be tagged and visible through the magnetic scanning device," he replied. "The tag will also identify her as harmless to the body. Still, there may be attempts at rejection. If the attempts are forceful, she can be immediately extracted."

He went to a diagram on the wall that was labeled GENOME and pointed to various blobs. At least, that was what the drawings looked like to Amy. But her mother and Dr. Dave seemed to understand the diagram and what Devon was saying.

"This is chromosome four. Amy will enter here."

"That would be appropriate," Dr. Dave said.

"Why?" Amy asked.

"Genetic mapping has given us some indication of

the location and functions of genes," Dr. Dave explained. "There are twenty-three pairs of chromosomes in a human cell. Chromosome four contains genes associated with the development of intelligence."

"It's a good place to start," Nancy added. "You may be able to learn the whereabouts of the Plague gene there."

"Or you could read the DNA strand," Dr. Dave suggested.

"Now, that would be exciting," Nancy said. "To actually read the instructions that govern the making of a human body!"

She was talking as if Amy was about to go off on some fabulous adventure. As a scientist, that was probably how Nancy saw this mission. But where had her maternal protectiveness disappeared to?

Mr. Devon was now pointing to another blob. "When you have the Plague gene, you will bring it to chromosome eighteen. These are the genes that control facial muscles. You will be able to force Tasha's features to present a signal, so that we will know you are ready to be extracted."

"What kind of signal?" Amy asked.

"Make her smile," her mother suggested.

As the three adults continued to talk, Amy withdrew into her own thoughts. She'd been involved in so many bizarre experiences, so many seriously dangerous tasks and terrifying events. And she'd felt fear before. But never like this. She couldn't take her eyes off Mr. Devon, but she knew that watching him wouldn't reveal anything. A clone was an exact replica. There was no way of knowing if this was the original Mr. Devon, the man who had saved her in the past.

For a long time, she had thought the original Mr. Devon was dead. She'd thought she'd seen his body behind the wheel of a car, back when she escaped from Wilderness Adventure two years ago. She didn't learn he'd been cloned till over a year later, when she encountered numerous Devons on the island. Were any of the clones good guys? Had the original Devon been a clone too? It was all totally confusing.

"Amy!"

Her mother's voice jerked her out of her meditations. "Amy, you need to be listening!"

"I *am* listening," Amy lied.

Nancy turned to the others. "Could you give us a moment alone?"

"There is no time to lose," the Devon person declared. "The patient is weak. If she dies before the gene is retrieved, it will no longer be viable for examination."

Amy searched his face. Had she just been given a

clue? The real Mr. Devon knew Tasha. Would he refer to her as "the patient" instead of using her name?

But now Dr. Dave was urging Devon out of the lab, as Nancy had requested, and Amy couldn't study his expression. Her mother took both of her hands in her own.

"Darling, you know I wouldn't allow you to do anything that would endanger your life."

"Mom, don't you think being reduced to the size of a gene is kind of borderline dangerous?"

Nancy looked serious. "I know it must sound frightening. But as a scientist, I know that this is manageable. It won't be easy. You may have extreme difficulty finding the faulty gene and bringing it to a place where it can be extracted. It's quite possible that you will fail. But you'll survive. We'll be watching you every second, and if anything becomes threatening, we will withdraw you immediately." She smiled. "For once, I'll actually be able to keep my eye on you. You'll be safer inside Tasha's genome than in your own bedroom."

Personally, Amy would much rather find herself back in her own bedroom. "But Mom . . . what about Mr. Devon?"

"Mr. Devon?"

"Do you *trust* him?"

"Of course I trust him," Nancy said. "He's always been there for us. Amy, you remember Dr. Jaleski."

Amy's hand went automatically to the crescent moon that hung from a silver chain around her neck. "Of course I do." She had met the former director of Project Crescent only twice before he died. His death hadn't been due to natural causes. He'd been murdered by the organization to keep him from revealing what he knew about it. But in the short time Amy had known him, she'd felt a special love for the grand-fatherly man.

After Dr. Jaleski's death, his daughter had presented Amy with the crescent moon pendant, saying that he'd made it himself for Amy. She wore it all the time.

"Back when you were twelve and Mr. Devon showed an interest in you, I was concerned. But Dr. Jaleski told me I could trust him. So I did, and I still do."

"But how do you know he's the real Mr. Devon?" Amy wanted to ask. But she couldn't. Because then she would have to explain to her mother experiences that she'd kept to herself, for her mother's safety.

The door opened, and the two men returned. "It is time," Mr. Devon said. Behind them, two orderlies were wheeling Tasha in on a gurney.

Amy heard someone else out in the hallway.

"Wait! I have to see Amy!"

Dr. Dave barred Eric from entering the lab. "I'm sorry, you can't come in here," he said. "Only authorized personnel are allowed."

"Just give her a message," the boy cried out. "Tell her thanks, okay? Tell her—tell her I love her!"

Amy was so shocked, she almost forgot what she was about to do. Even when they had been boyfriend and girlfriend, Eric hadn't been able to bring himself to say those words. Of course, this was a very emotional moment. Maybe he didn't even mean it the way it sounded. On the other hand, she was getting a pleasant little tickling sensation on the back of her neck.

She tried to hold on to the good feelings as she was guided into the device. It looked like one of those huge X-ray machines, the kind where the patient lies down on a platform that moves into an enclosed capsule. Tasha lay next to her.

Amy gazed at her best friend's face. How many times had the girls been side by side in twin beds at each other's homes? Hundreds, maybe thousands of times. This could be one of those mornings, when Amy woke up first and saw Tasha sleeping beside her.

Suddenly Amy wasn't quite as frightened as she had been. She wanted more of those mornings, and this was the only way she could have them. She would save her friend, and there would be many sleepovers in the future.

"Are you ready?" Devon asked.

How could anyone be ready for something like this? But Amy managed to say, "Yes." Her mother squeezed her hand. There was a mechanical humming.

The platform began to move, carrying Amy into the capsule.

f**5**ve

Everything went dark. The only sound was the humming of the machine. Amy steeled herself for strange and uncomfortable sensations.

It wasn't painful. The capsule was spinning, but it was going so fast that she didn't feel dizzy. She realized that she no longer felt the cold, hard metal of the platform. She simply had a sense of floating, as if in a pool of water or in space.

Now there were no sounds at all. There was light, but nothing to see. And nothing to touch or smell. It was as if her mind alone existed, without any physical body surrounding it. She had no arms or legs, no tongue or teeth . . . but she was alive, she existed. She could *think*.

She became aware of a force, the sensation of being pushed. She thought she might be leaving one environment and entering another. The light around her took on a rosy hue. It was misty—she was moving through pink clouds. The fact that she knew they were pink meant that she could see. There were sounds, too. Nothing she could identify, but ripples and spurts of uneven noise. The noise would stop, start, change in tone and volume—much like a conversation.

And there were shadows moving before her eyes. She wasn't alone. The shadows were real, existing just the way she existed. But the shadows were not exactly like her. They were different.

No—they were alike. *She* was different. She didn't belong there. She was a stranger in a strange land, an intruder, and she didn't think she was welcome. Because the shadows were gathering and moving toward her. And they didn't feel friendly.

She realized she was capable of movement. She could retreat from the advancing shadows and move sideways behind a thick cloud. From this position, she could no longer see the shadows, so she assumed they could no longer see her.

She assumed they were genes. Would she be able to

communicate with them? If all had gone according to plan, and she was actually in chromosome four, then these were genes that determined intelligence. Tasha was definitely intelligent, there was no doubt about that. Perhaps Amy would be able to convince them that she was no threat.

She sensed a noise behind her and moved in that direction. The sound came from a shadowy form. Like those that had come toward her, this form was amorphous, without any defined features. But Amy felt that it was alive, and she sensed no threat from it.

Amy spoke. It wasn't actual speaking, of course—it was more mental, but it felt like speaking, like an attempt to communicate.

"Hello. I'm not here to do any harm. I'm looking for a particular gene. Could you give me some directions?"

She knew she was transmitting something, but apparently, this wasn't a successful form of communication. There was no response from the gene.

She tried again. "There's a bad gene. It's hurting this body. Can you help me find it?"

Still no response.

"Can you understand me?" she asked. That was when she began to sense something coming from the form—not a communication, but an emotion. Something like fear. It was backing away from her.

Another form had entered her range of vision. Instinctively, Amy knew that it had a completely different nature from the thing in front of her. It approached with a confident aura, emitting a sense of importance. With its appearance, the first gene scurried away.

The second gene spoke. "Don't try to communicate with that one. It's a squatter." The tone was dismissive.

"What is a squatter?" Amy asked.

"A stupid, worthless remnant of a gene that has no function. It probably couldn't even understand what you were saying."

"But you do understand?" Amy asked.

"Certainly. I am a working gene. I have a role. What are you, some sort of medication? We don't need you. There is nothing to correct in this chromosome."

"No," Amy said, "I'm not a medication. I am a person. A human being. Do you know what that is?"

Now the gene's tone became haughty. "Of course I know what that is. Don't *you* know who you are talking to? I am a gene. I am part of the essence of a human being. What are you doing here?"

"This body is being threatened by a defective gene. It's causing a disease that will kill this human being if it isn't removed. I'm looking for it, to get it out of the body."

"I can assure you, the defective gene is not in *this* chromosome," the form declared.

"It could be hiding from you," Amy suggested.

"Impossible. This is chromosome four. The inhabitants of this chromosome are among the most intellectually astute groups in the genome. We would know if one of us was operating in some way that could hurt the body."

The gene's attention was distracted by a shadowy movement. "Get away, move along," the gene ordered, and the shadow ran away.

"Who was that?" Amy asked.

"Another stupid squatter."

"I don't understand," Amy said. "If this chromosome is devoted to intelligence, why are there so many stupid genes?"

"Squatters are everywhere. We can't get rid of them."

"If they have no job, what are they doing in the body?" Amy asked.

"Nothing, just taking up space. According to the historians in chromosome thirteen, they once had functions. But as the human organism evolved over millions of years, the role they played disappeared. That squatter you just saw . . . perhaps he was once responsible for wagging the tail of the human body—

which no longer has a tail. Now that so-called gene has nothing to do. It's utterly worthless, it serves no purpose, and it gets in the way of genes with functions."

Amy had an idea. "Is there any possibility that a squatter gene could be causing this disease?"

"No. Squatters are incapable of causing any real harm. They don't have the intelligence to do anything significant. If the disease that is killing this body is genetic, then it is caused by a working gene."

"And I have to find it," Amy said. "And get it out of the body."

"That won't be easy," the gene told her. "There are millions of working genes in a body."

Millions of working genes in twenty-three chromosomes—it was a daunting prospect. "There must be some way to narrow the search," she said. "A gene that wants to damage a body—isn't there one particular chromosome where it could do its work more easily? Where it might not be so conspicuous?"

"It's possible," the gene admitted. "In chromosome twelve, for example, are the genes which deal primarily in body assembly. Bodies change, so it's conceivable that the jobs there change too. But there are many other chromosomes that could accommodate a hostile gene. And you may not get very far in your exploration. Even though you may have no intention of harming the body, there are genes that will not recognize you as harmless and will assume you are a threat. You will be rejected."

Amy remembered what Devon had told her. "I'm supposed to be wearing a tag that identifies me as harmless," she said. Or had Devon lied to her about that?

Apparently not. "Yes, I can see that," the gene replied. "But as I told you, I am among the more astute genes. Others will not recognize this tag. You need a genetic marker which will allow you to pass from chromosome to chromosome without being rejected."

"Okay," Amy said. "How do I get one of these markers?"

The haughty tone was back. "It's not so easy. We do not simply hand them out to every foreign element that comes inside."

Amy envisioned the markers as something like green cards, which permitted immigrants to live and work in the United States legally. She imagined every country had a card or visa, or something similar, that would prove that an immigrant was not an illegal alien. Maybe that was how she should view Tasha's body—as a country she was visiting. She would need to know the laws of this country, the rules and regulations, so that she wouldn't do anything wrong. More than that—she needed to know the habits, the culture, the manners, so that she wouldn't offend the residents.

She spoke more humbly. "Do you know how I can apply for a marker?"

"I suggest that you go to chromosome eighteen. This is where genetic engineering is conducted, and they will be most accustomed to seeing foreign elements such as yourself."

"Thank you," Amy said politely. "Could you show me how to get there?"

The gene spoke with disapproval. "Did you not study a genetic map before undertaking this mission?"

Amy remembered the diagram Devon had been pointing to. "I guess I wasn't paying much attention."

Amy could imagine the gene's expression—if the gene had had a face. Like a schoolteacher who learned that a student hadn't prepared for a test. Or a Parisian who discovered that a tourist didn't know the difference between the Right Bank and the Left Bank.

"I will direct you," the gene said, relenting. "But I recommend that you learn the genome's network of connections."

"I will," Amy promised. She wondered if there were any genetic newsstands that sold maps.

s i x 6

Unfortunately, Tasha's genome wasn't Paris or New York. There were no souvenir shops offering postcards and street maps. If there was a subway system, Amy didn't see any signs. She followed the gene out of chromosome four and found herself moving along a maze of roads branching off and leading to other chromosomes. They didn't seem to lie in sequential order. She passed chromosome twenty-one, she saw chromosome two, then seven . . .

Although she didn't know what she was doing or where she was going, she wasn't frightened. She was fascinated. Sight had a whole different meaning here. It wasn't as if each chromosome held a neon sign proclaiming its number. But they had been marked in such a way that she could perceive their numbers through some sense she couldn't identify. A sort of strange but clear awareness.

Chromosome twelve . . . the gene had told her that body assembly occurred there. According to the gene, there was a possibility that the Plague gene could be operating out of that chromosome. But she was supposed to go to chromosome eighteen first, for her marker.

Here she was now, right in front of the chromosome that might contain the gene that was killing Tasha. She really didn't want to waste time running around in search of an identification badge. She decided to move directly into twelve.

This chromosome looked pretty much like the last one. The same rosy mist, the same blurry blobs moving around. She wondered how she would recognize the gene responsible for the Plague when all the genes looked alike.

A band of them was coming toward her now, just like in the last chromosome, and this group didn't seem any more welcoming. She tried to communicate.

"It's okay. Don't worry, I'm not an intruder," she began. But the group grew larger, and Amy started to get ominous vibrations from them. Looking around, she didn't see any thick mist to hide in. Moving backward, she began to feel uneasy. What did *rejection* actually mean, anyway?

"Really, I'm here to help," she said weakly, but clearly they weren't impressed. She knew they were telling her to leave, and they made sure she got the message. An individual gene came forward.

"Come on, you're out of here."

"Just let me explain," Amy pleaded, but the blob wasn't interested. Also, it was stronger than she was.

Getting out was harder than getting in. The gene that escorted her bumped into other forms. Amy took advantage of the time to ask questions.

"Have you seen any suspicious genes around? There's a defective creep in here somewhere. It might not be in this chromosome, but it's somewhere in Tasha's body. I've got to find it or it'll kill her. You don't want her to die, do you? I mean, if she dies, you die, right? Watch out!" They'd just collided with some unidentifiable mass.

"This is where the body assembly goes on, isn't it?" Amy went on. "So, like, if there's something wrong with someone's body, the gene that's responsible for it is in here somewhere, right?"

Finally, the gene communicated with her. "There are

no genes in this chromosome that don't belong here. *You* could be trying to disrupt this body."

"But I'm *not*," Amy protested. "Hey, why is it taking so much longer to get out of this chromosome than it took to get in? I feel like we're going in circles. Do you know the way?" There was another collision. "Hey, can you see where you're going?" Something occurred to her. "Wait a minute, are you the gene that's responsible for Tasha's being nearsighted?"

The gene didn't actually confirm this, but it didn't argue, either, and Amy had an idea. "I'm supposed to go to chromosome eighteen to get a marker. That's where the genetic engineering goes on. Why don't you come with me? Maybe you can get fixed up and Tasha won't have to wear contacts or glasses anymore."

The gene was irritated, that was clear from its tone. "They have more important things to do in eighteen than fix mildly poor vision. Tasha isn't blind. All bodies have imperfections. Don't try to mess around with Tasha, her body's all right just the way it is. Now beat it!"

Once again, Amy found herself in the road network. She plowed ahead in search of chromosome eighteen. Obviously, she wasn't going to get very far without that marker.

Eventually, she spotted the right chromosome. Getting in was easy—and the feeling she got from the genes around her wasn't hostility. It was more like curiosity.

She realized that they were discussing her.

"It needs work. A lot of work."

"What function is it supposed to perform?"

"It's unclear. But it's not a squatter. There's too much intelligence."

"Wait a minute," Amy interjected. "I'm not a gene. I'm a miniaturized human, looking for a gene. It's a disease-causing gene."

"There are no disease-causing genes here," a gene told her firmly. "This is a highly industrious chromosome. Genes are corrected here, they are made better. You could be better. A *lot* better."

Amy wasn't insulted, even though she was being told she was in drastic need of improvement. She simply told the engineering genes that she needed some sort of marker, and the genes obliged. Now she could pass freely through all the chromosomes.

She made her way back to twelve. This time she got in, and she cornered the first gene she came into contact with.

"Do you have any idea where I could find this defective gene?" she asked. "There are twenty-three chromosomes and millions of genes. If I have to search every chromosome, it could take me a long time."

"The location of every gene is noted in the DNA code," the gene told her.

"Oh yeah? Can I see this DNA code?"

She could—but she couldn't read it. The symbols that composed the language were totally indecipherable to her. "Can you translate this for me?" she asked a gene.

"No. DNA codes are secret."

"No, they're not," Amy argued. "Back in the real world, scientists use DNA all the time to identify people and diseases."

"Genes do not reveal the DNA codes. Your so-called scientists have to decipher them."

"But I don't know how to do that!" Amy cried. "Don't you care about this body? Tasha could die! What kind of gene are you?"

The gene took the question literally. "My function has to do with the determination of body type."

That gave Amy some ammunition to attack the gene. "Well, for your information, Tasha hates her body type. She thinks she has a big rear end and large thighs, and she wants to be thin."

The gene was unimpressed. "Well, that's too bad for her. She's not meant to be thin."

"But she gets really depressed about it!"

"Tell her to get over it. I'm not going to change."

"You really don't care about her at all, do you?" Amy shot back. "Couldn't you get your big fat butt over to eighteen and get yourself fixed so Tasha could be happy?"

"There is absolutely nothing wrong with Tasha's body," the gene retorted. "Tasha should learn to be happy with her body the way it is. People have to learn to start accepting themselves and stop fiddling with their genes for stupid reasons. Now get out of here and find the gene that's *really* hurting Tasha."

The gene had a point.

se7en

Amy got a warmer reception in chromosome eleven, which wasn't a big surprise. This was the chromosome where the genes dealing with Tasha's personality operated. Amy had always thought Tasha had a lot going for her—smarts, good looks, and above all else, a sharp personality. Tasha had her ups and downs, but she was never dull. And one of her best traits was that she really cared about people.

But Tasha hadn't been expressing her personality much lately. It was impossible to care about anything when you were in a coma. So in chromosome eleven, Amy found a bunch of genes without a whole lot to do. They were more than willing to hang out with Amy and reminisce.

"She had a great personality, didn't she?" a gene asked Amy wistfully.

"She still does," Amy said staunchly. "She just can't show it. When she comes out of this coma, she'll be great again."

"Tell us about her personality," they urged her.

"You made her personality. You must know all about it," Amy said.

The questions kept coming. "But how does she come across?" "What do people think about her?" "How do they react to her?"

Amy tried to describe Tasha. "Lots of people love her. She lets her feelings show, so people know she's for real."

"That's because there's not a phony gene in this chromosome," one of the personality blobs stated.

"And she never shows off or acts superior," Amy continued. "People like that."

"I've given her humility," a gene said. "But I work closely with the gene that gives her confidence, so she doesn't let people walk all over her."

Privately, Amy wasn't sure the confidence gene did a particularly great job. Sometimes Tasha put herself down. On the other hand, at least she wasn't like some kids who were concerned only with themselves.

"She's interested in everybody. People like that about her. But they can get angry at her too. Because she can be stubborn, you know?"

"I keep her stubborn," one gene declared. "I give her the courage to stand up for what she believes in."

"Yeah, well, sometimes she can be *too* stubborn," Amy said.

There was a rumble of discontent among the genes. "So you're saying there's something wrong with her personality?"

"Oh no, nothing like that," Amy said hastily. "Nobody's perfect. Being stubborn is part of who Tasha is." And as she said that, she realized that being nearsighted and a little chubby was part of who Tasha was too. No, she wouldn't want to change any of Tasha's genes. Except one.

"I'm looking for a bad gene," she told them.

"There are no bad genes in this chromosome," one of the blobs answered.

"Well, it's hiding out *somewhere*," Amy said. "Can't you help me?"

But the personality genes were distracted. There was a yell of warning. "Squatters! Squatters!"

As Amy watched, masses of genes tore off in pursuit. She heard cries of "Out, out!" It was strange, seeing the essence of Tasha's personality doing something she couldn't imagine Tasha doing: throwing other beings out of her house. From what she understood, the squatters were jobless and not too bright, but maybe they were worse than that. She wasn't going to learn anything about them from these genes, though. They were too busy chasing the poor squatters.

So she moved out of chromosome eleven and followed a pathway into the next chromosome, which turned out to be nineteen. She stopped the first gene she saw.

"Excuse me, what goes on in this chromosome?"

"Disease prevention," the gene told her hurriedly before moving on.

Amy caught her breath—or at least, that was what she would have done if she'd been breathing normally. She wasn't quite sure how her respiration was working in this situation. But however it was displayed, her excitement was justifiable: This was the chromosome she needed.

She doubted the Plague gene would be hiding out here. Unless it was stupid or reckless, it wouldn't try to do its dirty work in a chromosome devoted to wiping out disease. But this chromosome held the genes that would know how to hunt it down. They would help her. They would know what a disease-causing gene looked like, how it would behave, how it could be destroyed—or at least, how it could be rendered powerless.

Right this moment, these genes were probably working to help Tasha regain her health. They certainly seemed very busy. In fact, a large number of them appeared to be on a rampage, rushing past Amy in a determined manner. And suddenly she knew they weren't just running around—they were chasing something. Her excitement grew. Maybe they *were* on the track of the Plague gene!

She followed a group of genes moving in unison and tried to maneuver herself into a position where she could see the object of the pursuit. What would they do to the Plague gene when they caught it? Would they squash it? Blast it to smithereens? If she got to it first, she'd tear it limb from limb—except that genes didn't have limbs. It didn't matter; the disease blob didn't stand a chance with thousands of good genes and a miniaturized human after it. Its days were numbered.

"Where is it?" she asked the gene closest to her.

"What do you mean, 'it'? There's more than one. I counted at least a dozen."

Amy was surprised. "A dozen Plague genes?"

"No. A dozen squatters."

"Squatters!" she cried in disappointment. "You're chasing squatters?" She couldn't believe it. But now she could see those fuzzy blobs scampering away from the mob. She could hear them squealing unintelligibly as they fled from the genes.

"Why are you wasting time chasing squatters?" Amy asked. "There's a Plague gene loose in this body! You've got a real disease to stop!"

But they paid no attention to her. They were completely preoccupied with rounding up the squatters. She couldn't quite figure out what they planned to do with them after that. Eject them from the chromosome? Put them in some special squatter prison? It was a while before she could communicate with the genes.

"So what's the deal with these squatters?" she asked one.

She got the same explanation she had received in the first chromosome she'd visited. How the squatters were all over the place, how they didn't work, how they didn't contribute anything to the body, how they had no function, no value . . .

"There are hundreds and thousands of them," the gene told her. "Perhaps a million. Utterly worthless things."

"I'm talking about these particular squatters, the

ones you're rounding up and putting away some-where," Amy said. "Did they break a law or something?"

"No," another gene replied. "But they don't *do* any-thing. They have no business just hanging around here."

Amy still didn't understand. "So what? They don't bother anyone. Why do you make such a fuss about them? Do they cause diseases?"

"A mutation could turn any one of them into a disease-carrying gene."

Now, *that* was new and interesting information. "How does that happen?"

"It just happens. No one understands it. Any one of those squatters could mutate into something that hurts this body. It's happened before."

"To Tasha?"

"Yes. If you are her friend, surely you have noticed that she has a physical defect."

Amy was bewildered. Tasha's weak vision wasn't considered a real defect. And Amy couldn't think of anything defective about her friend's body. Maybe it was something that couldn't be seen, something that was wrong with one of her internal organs.

"What is it?" she asked nervously. "What's her defect?"

"Her fingernails. They're weak. Her brittle finger-nails are the result of a genetic mutation."

Amy vaguely recalled Tasha complaining about how her nails broke easily. "That's a defect?"

"It's not normal. It's an example of what can go wrong when a squatter mutates."

She supposed that if one mutation could cause brittle fingernails, another could cause the Plague. Maybe one of these squatters was actually dangerous. But which one?

"I don't suppose you'd read the DNA for me and tell me where the gene that carries the Plague is hanging out."

The gene wouldn't even dignify her question with an answer. It moved away from Amy as if she was carrying a plague herself.

But at least now she had a clue. She had to search for a mutated squatter. That should narrow the search . . . at least down to a million.

e**8**ght

In chromosome nineteen, the disease prevention genes continued to round up squatters.

The squatters weren't going along with the project willingly. There were sounds that Amy understood to be squeals of fear and protest as the squatters ran from the genes or tried to escape the tight circles the genes formed around them. But they didn't fight back or try to defend themselves. Escape seemed to be their only option.

It was interesting that she could now tell the genes from the squatters. Earlier they'd seemed identical.

Now they still looked alike—and yet she knew which were which. And not just because some were pursuing and others were fleeing. She didn't understand why or how, but there was a distinct difference. It wasn't their size—they were identical in that way. Maybe they looked different because the squatters didn't have the intelligence of the genes. Did smarter people look different from dumber people? Amy wasn't sure.

Obviously, the squatters didn't have the intelligence to do anything about their situation. Totally disorganized, they scurried around haphazardly, moving in all directions as they tried to avoid their pursuers. They seemed kind of pathetic to Amy, like ants trying not to be stepped on or flies avoiding a swat. They might slip through the grasp of a gene occasionally, but ultimately they were doomed.

It was hard to believe that one of those feeble beings could be responsible for something as deadly as the Plague. Amy could only guess that a mutation would have a dramatic effect on a squatter. She hoped the effect was visible so the evil mutated squatter would be easy to identify among the generally pitiful squatter population.

At least now she knew what her next step should be. She needed to start talking to squatters, to spot a mutation or see if she could pick up any clues as to where a mutated squatter might be lurking. Interviews wouldn't be possible while this rampage was going on, and it didn't look like it was going to end anytime soon. Watching carefully, she picked out three squatters traveling together, about to move out of the chromosome. In the chaos and confusion, the genes didn't see them. She took advantage of this and followed the squatters as they hurried away.

She was able to stay just behind them as they went into a nearby chromosome, number thirteen. It occurred to her that there couldn't be much contact between chromosomes—at least, no big roundup of squatters was going on in this particular place. Genes were moving about, doing whatever the genes here did. But there were a lot of them, thousands, and the three squatters she'd been following soon disappeared in the crowd.

Amy paused to consider her next move. Grabbing squatters at random and questioning them would only make them defensive and uncommunicative. She had to know more so she could narrow the field.

She looked around. What did she know about this place and its work? She recalled a gene in one of the other chromosomes telling her about a historian in chromosome thirteen. Maybe this was a good place to do some research. She stopped a passing gene.

"How can I find out the history of Tasha's genome?" she asked.

"You need to be more specific," the gene told her. "This chromosome is a library, a repository of knowledge. All human physiological history is here. What precisely are you interested in learning?"

"I'm trying to find a mutated gene," she said.

"We are not a detective agency," the gene responded. "We do not hunt down individual genes. Our work deals with the past. Human genetic history, this is our responsibility."

Still, Amy thought she could get some help here. "Okay, I want to know something about the past. The genes that existed during the Stone Age."

She was directed to one of the specialists in that area. That was when she realized that her perceptions had truly changed. She'd had a hint of this earlier, when she'd realized that she could distinguish a squatter from a gene. She couldn't define it precisely, but her insights were evolving. Genes still looked the same, but they began taking on characteristics that distinguished them. It was impossible for Amy to understand. The gene she was confronting, the specialist in Stone Age human physiology, was identical to every other gene she'd seen—and yet it was individual, unique. It was as if she'd developed an inner eye that could see beyond the obvious.

This gene was a scholar. It was older, wiser, and less arrogant than some of the genes she'd encountered. She knew she could get some straightforward answers, as long as she stayed within its field of expertise. This gene wouldn't be able to tell her where the Plague gene was—but it could provide her with information that would help her search.

"I want to know about a gene that caused a disease. It came from an alien exposure back in the Stone Age."

The gene understood. "The gene you're asking about became part of the human genome through interaction with another biological entity."

"Yes, exactly," Amy said. "I need to find out what happened to that gene."

Apparently, this library had the genetic version of online resources. The gene was able to provide instant answers.

"The gene in question was not nurtured," it told her. "Only two humans had contact with the beings who possessed the gene. As the human population evolved, the gene weakened. It became less and less capable of performing its function. Ultimately, it lost all power."

Amy knew what happened to genes that couldn't perform their work. "So it became a squatter. An out-of-work gene."

"Yes."

"Is there any way of figuring out *which* squatter? Does it have any distinguishing characteristics?"

"No. You don't need to find it. As I've told you, the gene no longer has any power."

"But that's just it," Amy said. "It got its power back. It mutated, and it's working again. It's making the disease in this body. I don't know how this happened."

"Mutations are common. There may be a hundred mutations in this body. Most of them are harmless."

"But this one isn't. It's killing the body."

"There are many mysteries in the human genome," the gene said. "For some reason, the DNA code has switched in this gene."

"So if I could read the DNA code, I could find out which gene is turned on, right?"

"Yes, that's correct."

"But I *can't* read the code!" Amy wailed. "And none of these genes will help me out!"

"The DNA code is a secret. Only working genes

can read it, and they are not permitted to communicate it."

"Not permitted by whom?" Amy demanded. "Is there some king gene who makes the rules around here?"

No, the gene answered, there was no king, no president, no chairgene in the genome. The only governing body was nature. Control came from the instructions in the DNA, and these instructions told the genes what they had to do. And only genes could read the instructions.

So Amy wouldn't get any answers in chromosome thirteen. Unless that happened to be where the Plague gene was hiding out.

That *was* a possibility. The genes of chromosome thirteen didn't seem terribly disturbed by the presence of squatters. At least, they weren't chasing them out. These squatters were ignored—which meant this would be a good chromosome for an evil squatter gene to operate in.

And Amy could interview squatters here. She could start playing detective.

Only, the squatters weren't ready to play along. She approached a group that seemed to be hanging out, and before she could even begin communicating with them, they ran away. She was sure it wasn't guilt that caused them to react this way. It was definitely fear.

Clearly, even in the relative safety of chromosome thirteen, the squatters didn't feel secure.

With the next squatter, she concentrated on being friendly and hoped she was getting the message across. "Please don't run away. I just want to ask you a question . . . ," she began.

The squatter didn't move. Encouraged, she continued. "Do you know where the Plague gene is?"

The squatter didn't reply. Maybe it was thinking. . . . No, there wasn't any thinking going on in this blob. She felt like she was trying to communicate with the dead.

A couple of other squatters hovered around, and Amy addressed them all. "I'm looking for the Plague gene." When that brought no response, she rephrased the statement. "I'm looking for a switched-on squatter. It's causing a terrible disease. Do you know where it could be hiding?"

Still nothing. She wondered if the squatters were like a gang, protecting one of their own. "This squatter, he's *bad*," she said. "You don't want to be his friend. I know you guys are out of work, and you're probably depressed about it, but hey, being unemployed isn't the worst thing in the world. It's better than being a criminal, right? You know what I mean?"

Clearly, they did not.

"Do you understand me? Are we speaking the same language?"

Finally, she got some little squeak that she took for a yes. "Then why don't you answer me?" She was getting frustrated. It was time to get tough.

"Look, I'm going to find this gene," she declared. "I'm taking it out of this body. It will be destroyed. And if I have to drag a few innocent squatters like you out with it, that's too bad. You won't survive either."

At least this threat got a response—but it wasn't exactly what she'd expected. The squatters backed away, making a new noise. It took some time before Amy could identify the sound.

They were *crying*. The wimpy squatters were afraid of her!

"But if you show me exactly who the Plague gene is, I won't have to do that," she assured them.

That didn't comfort them. They continued to wail. Her frustration reached a new level. "Just help me out! That's all I ask! If you take me to this Plague gene, I won't hurt you."

Finally, one of the blubbering squatters came forward. "We don't know who the Plague gene is."

"But you must know something! Can't you recognize a squatter with a new job?"

"No! We don't know anything."

Another squatter chimed in. "We're squatters, we're worthless."

Amy was stymied. They sounded so sincere, they had to be telling the truth.

"Don't hurt us!" they pleaded.

Then she thought of a way they could help her. They might be worthless squatters, but they were still genes—which meant they had an ability she didn't have.

She felt crummy doing it, but she had to take advantage of their fear. "Okay, I won't hurt you if you do something for me."

At least one squatter had the guts to argue. "How can we help you if we don't know anything? And we can't do anything either."

"You can read the DNA code and tell me what it says."

"We can't do that!" the squatter protested.

Amy groaned. "Oh, for crying out loud. Don't tell me you have to keep the DNA code secret. It doesn't even give you any instructions! Why can't you read it to me?"

There was a murmur among them. Finally, the gutsy one gave her an answer. "Because we can't read."

Others supported this. "We're not just unemployed."

"We have no abilities. We can't do any of the things the working genes do."

"We have no value."

"And we're really stupid."

So the genes hadn't been exaggerating. The squatters were really, truly, utterly worthless. They wouldn't be able to help at all.

nine

"Oh, this is great," Amy groaned. "This is just great."
Her sarcasm was lost on the squatters. She still sensed confusion and uncertainty. But their fear was passing. Other curious squatters joined them, and soon a small crowd had gathered around her.

She decided they weren't really so much like ants and flies. The squatters were more like dogs and cats, tame animals that were frightened by strangers but eventually could be coaxed into trusting them. Like sweet, dumb, harmless dogs—not the pit-bull variety.

They were still milling around her. She figured they were attracted by the fact that she wasn't pushing them away, that she'd even made the effort to talk to them. The big-shot working genes ignored them or persecuted them. The squatters were probably starved for affection or just some friendly attention. Amy had to feel sorry for them.

But what am I supposed to do now? she wondered in despair. The genes wouldn't help her, and the squatters couldn't. She didn't have an eternity to wander through the twenty-three chromosomes and question every gene that was functioning. And if there was no way to quickly recognize a recently mutated squatter—then . . .

"What chance do I have of finding the Plague gene before it kills Tasha?

"What is Tasha?"

It was a moment before she realized that a squatter was asking a question. She must have been speaking out loud.

"Tasha is the name of this body," she said, speaking slowly and carefully, as if explaining the situation to a four-year-old. "There is a bad gene in this body." Would the squatters understand the concepts of illness and death? She doubted it. "The bad gene is hurting Tasha. I am looking for the bad gene so I can make it stop hurting her."

Did they get it? She wasn't sure. She felt *something*

emanating from the squatters. Something emotional. Puppy-dog devotion?

She couldn't waste more time with them, though. She had to keep moving.

Entering chromosome eight was like walking into a copy shop—every gene was occupied with copying, replicating, transcribing. It looked like a lot of boring drudgery to her, but she supposed the human body required its own version of paperwork.

Maybe if their work was as boring as it looked, they wouldn't mind being interrupted. She approached a line of genes that appeared to be collating something.

"Excuse me," she began, and that was as far as she got.

"Beat it!" The gene's tone was mildly harsh, but definitely dismissive.

"Look, I just want to ask—"

"Get out of here!" Now the tone was clearly hostile. She was surprised. Most of the genes had been willing to talk to her.

Then she saw why they were greeting her like this. She was no longer conducting a one-person investigation. She had an entourage. That crowd of squatters had followed her into the chromosome, practically at her heels.

Amy had always wanted a pet, but Nancy had never

allowed her to have one. They required too much attention. Now Amy had a thousand pets. And if the genes were going to react like this, her squatter pets would be a liability.

"Hey, guys, you can't follow me around, okay? I'm busy, I'm on a mission."

Did they understand her? Clearly not. Unless they were just being stubborn—and she doubted they had the intelligence to make that kind of commitment. Whatever the reason, they stayed with her as she continued moving through chromosome eight.

Amy increased her speed to get ahead so the working genes wouldn't associate her with them. "Attention, attention, all you working genes, listen up. I need help. Can someone help me?" Some genes turned in her direction. "Can someone read the DNA code for me? Please, it's urgent!"

She would have thought they'd be dying for a break from their tedious labors. And she did get some attention, but it wasn't the kind she wanted.

The squatters had stuck to her. And the sight of all those squatters converging must have been a major annoyance. A cry went up among the working genes. "Get those squatters out of here!"

Amy was getting fed up with the genes' superior attitude. She planted herself between them and the squatters. "Hey, what's your problem?" she said to the genes. "They're not hurting you! They're not even getting in your way. Why do you have to run them out of your chromosome?"

She didn't get an answer. Her words didn't have any impact at all. The genes had moved into a pack, and they were heading toward the squatters. Amy expected the squatters to start squealing and running. But this time, instead of fleeing from the genes, they huddled together right behind her. It was as if they were expecting her to protect them.

And Amy decided to do just that. She was irritated with the genes, she felt sorry for the pathetic squatters, and she was frustrated with the fact that she hadn't accomplished anything. So she stood her ground and geared herself up to fight off the army of genes.

"I'm warning you!" she yelled. "You'd better not mess with me! I'm not any ordinary miniaturized human, I'm genetically engineered. I can take you on!"

Only, she couldn't. It wasn't until she felt the first gene smash into her that she understood. The second gene that ran her down served to confirm the realization. She couldn't stop them. The marker that she'd received in chromosome eighteen, the tag that told them she was harmless—it actually *made* her harmless. She had no special abilities here. She couldn't make a gene read the DNA code for her, she couldn't protect the squatters, she couldn't stop the genes from rolling over her. This made her realize something more depressing. Even if she eventually found the Plague gene, how was she going to force it out of the genome?

But she had a more immediate problem—getting away from the genes before they caused her actual damage. It was so humiliating, being chased from the chromosome like a nobody. But there she was, scrambling out of chromosome eight right along with the ordinary, pitiful squatters.

Once outside, she didn't know where to go next, and she didn't think it would matter. As long as the horde of squatters accompanied her, she wouldn't be welcome in any chromosome, and no gene would listen to her pleas for help.

If she begged to be left alone, would the squatters understand? Would they listen and obey? Would it make any difference?

"Ten."

A squatter had spoken. It was probably demonstrating how high it could count.

"That's nice," Amy said as she tried to decide what her next move should be.

"We should go to ten now." There was a murmur of agreement among the other squatters.

Amy turned in the direction of the squatter that had made the suggestion. "Chromosome ten?" she asked.

"Yes."

"Why? What happens in chromosome ten?"

"The genes deal with stress."

"Stress," Amy repeated. "You mean like worrying?"

"Yes. So we should go there now."

It was talking nonsense, but Amy humored it. "Why?"

"This body, this Tasha . . . you say it has an illness?"

"*She,*" Amy corrected the squatter. "Not 'it.' Tasha is a person, she has a sex."

"Sex?"

Briefly, she wondered if she should take them all for a visit to the X chromosomes, where she could tell them about X and Y and explain what made a person male or female. No, there wasn't any time for squatter education.

"Never mind, it's not important. What does worrying have to do with Tasha's illness?"

"A body that is sick will be under stress. So the genes in chromosome ten will know about the sickness."

Amy had to admit that the squatter was making a point. In fact, it was a logical conclusion. She was amazed. Was this a fluke, or did some of these squatters actually have some intelligence?

"That's a smart thing to say," she told it.

The squatter disagreed. "No, we are not smart."

Others chimed in. "We are stupid."

"We have no jobs."

"We are worthless."

Amy didn't argue. "I don't suppose any of you knows where this chromosome ten is."

"South." The squatter that spoke turned and began moving. The others followed. Amy hurried to catch up with the leader.

"Why south?" she asked.

"Because I have seen chromosome ten in the south."

"But how do you know which way is south?" Roaming around this genome, Amy had lost all sense of direction. And she had another thought. "How do you even know what *south* means?"

"I know south," the gene said. "That was my job. I told the body to go south. I worked in chromosome seven. Instinctive behavior."

She realized that this squatter must have been active in the era when prehuman creatures headed south as a natural response to the approach of winter. "You remember that?"

"Yes."

She turned to another squatter that was moving alongside her. "Do you remember what your job was?"

The squatter answered promptly. "Hair. I made hair grow."

"But people still have hair," Amy pointed out. "How come you're out of work?"

"I made hair on the back of the body," the squatter said.

Amy understood. Early humans had been covered with hair. There must have been a lot of work for hair genes to do back then. Some people still had hair on their back. Amy had seen men on the beach with lots of it. But people weren't covered with hair anymore. People didn't need it to keep warm, the way animals did.

"You must have been very important back then," Amy said.

"Yes, I had an important job," the squatter said. "I was very busy. But I'm not needed now. I was switched off a long time ago."

There was a wistful note in its voice. Human evolution had cost lots of genes their jobs.

Amy questioned another squatter about its past. She was told it had made teeth sharper. "I don't know why I was turned off," it said.

Amy suspected this had something to do with humans no longer needing to eat freshly killed animals. "Food isn't that hard to chew anymore," she told it.

"Yes, I thought that might be the reason," the squatter said sadly. "So now I am unemployed."

Amy reflected that it was too bad this squatter couldn't be switched on in the cafeteria at school so the students could chew the mystery meat. At least the former working gene could have a part-time job.

She reflected on something else, too. These squatters didn't communicate like stupid people or immature kids. Were they really as dumb as the employed genes said they were? They remembered so much, and they expressed themselves perfectly well.

She shared her thoughts with them. "You know, you sound pretty intelligent to me. Just because you're unemployed doesn't mean you're stupid."

"No, we're stupid," a squatter said. "We do nothing."

This time, Amy argued. "Just because your jobs are obsolete doesn't mean you're stupid."

"We're stupid," the squatter repeated, and the others added their comments.

"We are worthless."

"We have no value."

They spoke with such conviction that Amy knew she couldn't change their attitude. Of course, it wasn't surprising that they felt this way. The working genes belittled them, ignored them, treated them like dirt. No wonder they thought they were stupid. That was what they were told. They were just living up to expectations—or living down to them.

What these guys needed was a healthy dose of self-esteem. Like a job to do. But there wasn't much Amy could do about that. It wasn't as though she could urge them to start doing their old jobs. Even if she could read the DNA code and figure out a way to switch the squatters back on, that could be problematic. When Tasha came out of her coma, she wouldn't be too pleased to find herself covered with hair.

ten 10

Amy couldn't shake the squatters. In fact, more joined the group as she made her way to chromosome ten. By the time she arrived at her destination, she felt like she was leading an army.

Unfortunately, that was how the genes of chromosome ten perceived the squatters too. She sensed that alarms were going off, and all activity in the chromosome suddenly ceased.

If she hadn't already known that this chromosome dealt with stress, she would have guessed it from their reception. The feeling of tension was high, and she could practically smell the anxiety in the air. This was a very nervous bunch of genes.

"What do you want?" one of them asked. Amy could have sworn its voice was quivering. She couldn't understand why they seemed on edge. The squatters weren't hostile. If anything, they were too meek and submissive.

Amy started to explain. "I'm looking for a squatter that's just been turned on. Are you aware of a gene that's making this body sick?"

"A squatter has been activated?" She was aware of a jumble of voices speaking fearfully about the danger implicit in this action. A gene asked, "How did this squatter get switched on?"

"The DNA code instructions, I guess. If one of you could help me read the code, I could find out where this gene is."

"And turn on some other squatters while you're at it," a gene declared.

"Oh, I wouldn't do that," Amy assured them. "I wouldn't even know how!"

"We don't believe you! You come here with an army of squatters ready to do battle."

"They don't want to do battle! They don't know how to fight. They don't know how to do anything!"

The gene countered this. "Not now, they don't. Because they're switched off. If you were able to read ~~~~ DNA code, you might figure out a way to turn them all back on!"

Another gene piped up. "This body could grow a tail! Or develop gills!"

Amy tried to make them see reason. "We're talking about my best friend here. Believe me, there's no way I would do anything that might give her a tail. I don't know how the Plague gene got switched on, all I know is that I have to stop it before it does more damage. You guys should understand. You're too stressed out *not* to know you're dealing with an illness, right?"

There was no response. And then Amy realized that while she'd been making her little speech, the genes of chromosome ten had encircled her group. Now *she* was beginning to feel anxious.

"Look, don't worry, we're no threat to you. We don't want to fight you. What's the point in that?"

A gene spoke in a high-pitched voice. "We know what you want. You want to rule. You're going to empower these squatters and take over the body."

"That's crazy!" Amy protested. She was beginning to think the squatters were more intelligent than these genes. But the squatters, with their low self-esteem, weren't thinking along those lines. They allowed the genes to close in on them without protest. They were used to being pushed around.

Amy had no superstrength, and she knew the squatters wouldn't provide any support. "Okay, okay," she said, relenting. "We'll leave. If you don't want to help, we're out of here. We'll go to another chromosome. There have got to be genes with some guts somewhere."

It was probably foolish of her to taunt them. They didn't move. "All right, I'm sorry I called you gutless wimps! Could we just leave, please? This body's in danger. There's no time to play games. We need to go find the evil gene!"

Maybe she should have used a singular personal pronoun. After all, the squatters weren't actually going to help her find the Plague gene. But she'd become used to their company, and was almost feeling as if they were all part of a Save Tasha team.

But the genes around them had created a barrier. It dawned on Amy that her team wasn't going anywhere. And now they were being physically pushed in a direction that had apparently been agreed upon by the genes.

"Hey, you don't have to get rough. We can leave on our own," Amy declared.

"You're not leaving," one of the genes told them. "We don't want you to disrupt the work of other chromosomes."

Now Amy was really feeling stressed. "Where are you taking us?" she asked uneasily.

"To the place where all troublemakers go. You will be imprisoned in a DNA molecule until we are given instructions."

"What? You can't put us in jail! We haven't done anything wrong! I demand to see a lawyer!"

If she hadn't been in such dire circumstances, she would have laughed at how ridiculous she sounded. But everything about this place was so unreal, it seemed appropriate to get dramatic.

She tried to push back. On her own, she couldn't provide much resistance, and she certainly couldn't break the bond of the genes. If only she could make her squatters behave like a team . . .

"C'mon, squatters! Push them back! Break out!"

But the team concept was all in her imagination. There was no fight in the squatters. They'd gone limp and were making no attempt to resist the force of the genes. They were all pushed onto a higher level, a platform or bridge or something. Mist engulfed them, and she could barely make out the genes.

But she could sense that the degree of tension among the genes had dropped. They were a lot more relaxed now.

"You are imprisoned," a gene intoned. "Any attempt at escape is futile. You cannot leave the molecule." They disappeared beyond the mist.

Amy looked around. The fog that surrounded her and the squatters had to be the genetic version of a jail cell. Within the clouds, symbols were floating. They seemed like letters, or words, but in a language and an alphabet she couldn't recognize.

"Is that the DNA code of instructions?" she asked the squatters.

There was a general murmur that she took as a yes. She stared at the symbols and concentrated on them. In real life, she'd always been able to learn a new language rapidly. But that was because of her superior genes. Here, with no superiority at all, the symbols didn't begin to take on any meanings. She had a sinking suspicion that all the time in the world wouldn't be enough to enable her to learn this language. And she didn't have all the time in the world.

Don't panic, she warned herself. *Think.* There's got to be a way out.

A symbol passed just before her eyes. She reached

out and touched it, and a piece seemed to drop off. That was interesting. Maybe if she fiddled around with these symbols, she could make the DNA change an instruction?

"I don't think you should do that," one of the squatters said.

She wasn't surprised to hear that recommendation. These squatters were so passive, such wimpy do-nothings, they'd be shocked by the notion of trying to get out of this mess. They'd be perfectly willing to sit here and rot in jail.

"I'm trying to change the instructions so we can get out of here," she told them.

"But you can't read the instructions. If you change something, you could hurt Tasha."

With horror, she realized the squatter was right. It would be like misreading the instructions for hooking up a VCR to a TV. Misread one line, attach two wrong wires—and nothing would work. Had she just done something to Tasha? Could she have caused her best friend to become blind or paralyzed?

"Don't touch the symbols!" she called out. She just hoped she hadn't already done any damage.

"We won't touch anything," a squatter said.

"We won't do anything," another added. "We *can't* do anything."

Amy sighed. It was clear the squatters felt their existence had no meaning. Even if she could free them, what good would it do? They'd just remain in Tasha, doing nothing, until Tasha's body ceased to exist.

They didn't seem to care that that could happen very soon.

eleven

Amy had no idea how long they'd been sitting in prison. Minutes? Hours? Days? She wondered if her mother, Dr. Dave, and Mr. Devon were watching, waiting for her to find a way out. They must be so disappointed in her. Still, the fact that she hadn't been extracted was good—it meant that Tasha was hanging on.

But maybe they *couldn't* extract her, now that she was imprisoned in a DNA molecule! The thought was too overwhelming to contemplate. Wildly, she turned to the closest squatter. Why wasn't it reacting to this situation? Had they all been beaten down so much that they didn't have any anger left in them? There wasn't even any sign of despair. The squatter was actually singing!

Or humming, or something like that. It wasn't much of a tune—more like a listless, automatic chanting. A prayer, maybe? Did genes and squatters have a religion?

Amy couldn't understand what the squatter was chanting. It was all gibberish to her. But apparently it was common knowledge to all the squatters. Another picked up the tune and joined in, then another. Soon a lot of them were chanting the same nonsense sounds.

Looking for anything to take her mind off her predicament, Amy interrupted the closest squatter. "What are you singing?"

The squatter paused. "I don't know."

"You don't know?"

"It's just there."

"In your head?" she asked.

"I don't have a head."

This conversation wasn't going anywhere. But now, despite her fear, Amy was getting more and more curious. The chanting had become a chorus of thousands. She addressed the group.

"What's going on? How do you all know this song?"

One of them answered. "Because it's there."

"There *where*?"

A squatter pointed into the mist. "There."

Amy had no idea what the squatter was talking about. All she saw was the mist. And the symbols floating around in it.

She frowned. "The symbols? Are you singing those symbols? Are they words, or notes, or something like that?"

No one could answer her. So she answered herself. "It's the code! You're reading the DNA code!"

"We can't read," a squatter said.

But Amy didn't buy that. "Yes, you can. That's what you're doing right now. You're all reading the symbols!"

Suddenly it made sense. They'd been told they were worthless, that they couldn't do anything. For generations and generations, they'd believed this. But with the words or letters or notes or whatever those symbols were passing right before whatever they had for eyes, the natural instinct took over—and they automatically read them.

"Tell me what you're reading," she begged them. "Tell me, in a way I can understand."

It was all there, in black and white. Every instruction

to every gene in Tasha's body. "I see it," a squatter whispered in awe. "I know it. I'm reading the instructions." All the orders, all the messages that told the genes what to do—the squatters could understand all of them. They could identify the symbols that indicated whether genes were switched on or off. They could read, every one of them. It wasn't magic—they'd always been able to read. They'd never lost the skill. They'd just been made to *think* they had.

She was almost afraid to ask. "Does it say if an old gene's been switched back on recently?"

A chorus of voices answered in the affirmative. A squatter, an unemployed gene just like them, had been turned on. Something was happening right now in Tasha's body, something that had only happened to people millions of years ago.

"It's the Plague gene," Amy whispered. "It *has* to be. Where is it?"

Squatters answered in unison. "Chromosome seven."

So that was where she had to go—chromosome seven. There was only one problem—how to get there? She was trapped, locked up in a molecule. She was imprisoned, she was in jail.

Or was she?

Squatters had been told they couldn't read, so they

didn't even try. They'd been told they were in jail—and they believed it. But what if it wasn't true?

"We can leave," Amy announced. "Never mind what those genes said. We're not locked in here. We can leave if we want. Just *believe* it. Let's go! We can leave!"

And she wasn't very surprised when they did.

twelve 12

Once they were all out of the DNA molecule, the squatter who used to work in chromosome seven took the lead. Amy and the thousand other squatters followed closely behind.

Even in her excitement, during the brief dash to the chromosome, Amy thought she sensed something different about her squatters. There was something in their mood—a determination, a feeling of purpose. She was glad to see this. But she wanted to go into chromosome seven alone. With hordes of squatters accompanying her, she feared she might be considered a danger. But how could she tell them to stay back? They were so thrilled to have something to do!

So Amy didn't try to stop them. It wouldn't have done any good if she'd tried. They were on a mission now too.

Word of their arrival had spread, and the genes of chromosome seven were waiting for them. *Not* with open arms. Amy and the squatters were actually barred from entering.

"You have no business here," the gene at the entrance announced. "You have no business anywhere. We don't want unemployed genes in our chromosome. We have no space for squatters."

Amy was all set to go into her explanation when a squatter spoke up. "Seems you've got plenty of space for an evil killer."

"What are you talking about?" the gene demanded.

"There's a gene in the chromosome that's causing a disease," the squatter reported. "We're here to get it out."

Amy felt warm all over. The squatter was sounding like a team member.

"That's ridiculous," the gene said. "There are no bad genes here."

How many times had Amy heard this since she'd entered the genome? And she still didn't know how to respond. "Just let me in so I can talk to them," she pleaded.

"No."

Amy knew she didn't have to accept that. "You think you can stop us?" she yelled. "Just because you think so doesn't make it true. C'mon, squatters!" Together they charged forward.

But all the determination and belief in the world was not going to make up for the fact that these squatters were out of shape. Lack of work and exercise for millions of years had weakened them. There were only about a hundred genes blocking their entrance—but that was enough. They were stronger than a thousand squatters.

"Now get out of here!" the genes ordered them.

Amy couldn't believe this. To be so close to the Plague gene and not be able to confront it was unbearable. But they wouldn't listen to her pleas, and even with a thousand supporters, she couldn't force her way in.

Was this it, then? Had she reached the end of the road?

Then a squatter spoke. "Do you know me?"

The gene glanced briefly at the speaker. "No. I don't socialize with bums."

"I wasn't always unemployed," the squatter said. "In fact, I worked here, in this chromosome. I led the body south for the winter."

"Congratulations," the gene said sarcastically. "Go work in a bird's genome. For your information, bodies don't have to go south for the winter anymore. They have heat. They wear coats."

"I know that," the squatter replied. "But I know how this chromosome operates. When I was working here, I didn't feel the cold. I knew it was winter by instinct."

"Yeah, yeah, what else is new?" the gene sneered. "We all work by instinct in here."

"Oh, really? I guess your instincts are pretty dull now."

Now the gene was offended. "My instincts are as sharp as they've ever been."

"I doubt that. If your instincts are so sharp, how come you haven't spotted the Plague gene by now?"

"Because the Plague gene isn't here!"

"Yes, it is." In one voice, the thousand squatters began to chant the instructions they'd read in the DNA code. When they finished, the hundred genes from chromosome seven were silent.

Finally, the guard gene spoke up. "Come in."

thirteen 13

Amy could only hope that the genes weren't exaggerating about their instincts. There were thousands of workers milling around, and to Amy's eyes, they all looked pretty much alike. No one was wearing a badge that read HELLO, MY NAME IS PLAGUE.

The working genes moved through the chromosome, looking and watching. The squatters stayed close, and Amy trembled with excitement.

Suddenly, the genes stopped. Instinct had kicked in. They were all looking in the same direction. "There's your gene."

They spoke with such conviction, Amy didn't even ask if they were sure. She had to trust their instinct.

"It doesn't belong here," a gene said. "It's evil. We'll throw it out."

"No, wait," Amy said. "That's not going to help the body. It will just drift into another chromosome and hide out there until it finishes its dirty work. I have to take it out of the body altogether. I'll hold it down, give a signal, and the two of us will be extracted."

"How do you give the signal?" a gene asked.

Amy thought back to the instructions she'd been given. "I have to get the gene into chromosome eighteen. Then I get the genes in there to make a smile on Tasha's face. That will alert the people outside the body that I'm ready."

"And do you think I'm just going to stand still and wait for you to do that?"

Amy turned. She was face to face with the Plague gene. Of course, there was no face, and it didn't have an expression. Yet Amy knew that it was mocking her. It wasn't even trying to deny what it was.

It had to know she had no special powers here. But the genes and squatters rallied around. The Plague gene was surrounded.

"Bring it to chromosome eighteen," Amy instructed them.

But now something else was happening. A shrill alarm went off, and the genes were suddenly alert.

"What's going on?" Amy asked.

"It's the body! Something's wrong."

The Plague gene laughed. "*Very* wrong. It's dying!"

The squatters were yelling, "Take it out *now*! There's no time to bring it to eighteen!"

"I can't give the signal here!" Amy wailed. "I have to make Tasha smile. These genes don't control facial muscles!"

"But we control instinct," a gene reminded her. "If you say something funny, we'll laugh, and Tasha will smile."

The Plague gene was still laughing. "Brilliant idea. Do you know what will happen if this human gives the signal? You'll be extracted from the body right along with us! And you know what will happen then?" The Plague gene roared with laughter. "The body loses a whole bunch of genes. I won't kill her. *You'll* kill her! And you'll be dead too!"

Amy went cold all over as the horrible irony of the situation hit her. The genes understood it too. They released their hostage and moved away from it. And the Plague gene continued to laugh.

Amy threw herself at it. She concentrated with all her might on believing in her strength. But all the confidence in the world couldn't change the reality of the situation. She didn't have the power. The gene pushed her off and stood alone.

But the gene wasn't alone for long. The army of squatters took Amy's place. They might not have been strong enough to battle a hundred genes, but they could take one on easily. The Plague gene was pinned down.

It still didn't show any fear. "You're coming out with me," it warned the squatters.

"But the body won't die," a squatter told it. "We don't do anything for Tasha. She won't suffer at all if she loses us."

"But you will," the Plague gene said. "*You* will cease to exist. You'll die outside the body. Isn't that right, human girl?"

Amy couldn't lie to her squatters. A sob welled up inside her. "Yes, that's right. Get off the creep, guys."

The squatters didn't budge. "Give the signal," they told her. "Make Tasha smile."

"No, I can't let you do that!" Amy cried out. "You don't have to sacrifice yourselves."

But a squatter spoke for all of them. "Why not? Our

lives here have no meaning. We have no jobs, we have no value."

"Stop that!" Amy yelled. "You're not worthless! You're not stupid!"

"But we have nothing to do," the squatter said. "Let us give ourselves for Tasha. At least our death can have some meaning. We can make a contribution."

"Hey, are you jerks nuts or something?" the Plague gene demanded. For the first time, Amy detected a note of fear.

The alarms were louder now. "Hurry, get it out!" a gene called. "The body can't last much longer!"

A squatter addressed Amy. "Make her smile! Tell a joke!"

Panic overcame her. A joke, a joke . . . *what* joke? The last thing she felt like doing was telling a joke. What kind of joke would make Tasha instinctively smile? Why had her mind suddenly gone blank? There had to be a joke in there somewhere!

She was desperate. She had to use the only thing that came to her. Turning to the instinct genes, she asked, "What's black and white and red all over?" She didn't wait for them to ask "What?" Throwing herself onto the pile of squatters holding the Plague gene down, she screamed out the answer.

"A sunburned zebra!"

And suddenly she was twisting around in a whirlwind of pink clouds and lights . . . she was floating, hanging in space . . . and she felt herself being pulled away. Spinning . . . expanding . . .

. . . until she opened her eyes and found herself back inside the capsule.

fourteen

The capsule opened. Stiffly, Amy crawled out. "Is she okay? Is Tasha going to be all right?"

Then she saw Tasha, in the same place she'd last seen her, on the gurney. Tasha's chest was moving up and down—a good sign. And Nancy Candler was smiling, nodding—another good sign. Amy felt relief wash over her.

She had less than a minute to enjoy the feeling. Two strong hands grabbed her shoulders. And suddenly, she was gripped in a hold she couldn't break. It took a few seconds for the identity of her abductor to register.

"Mr. Devon! What—what's going on?"

Nancy Candler's smile had disappeared, and Dr. Dave was clearly stunned.

"What are you doing?" Nancy shouted.

"I am holding your daughter hostage," Devon said in a clear, controlled voice. "Give me the gene or I take her away. And if I take her away, it is quite possible you will never see her again."

"Are you crazy?" Nancy cried out. "Let her go! What's wrong with you?"

Amy struggled to free herself, but to no avail. She couldn't break his grip. Didn't she have her powers back?

Accusations of insanity didn't bother this Devon clone. His voice remained calm. "Just give me the test tube, Ms. Candler, and no one will be hurt. I want that gene."

Dr. Dave found his voice. "The Plague gene? You want to take the Plague gene? But—but why?"

"So that I can bring it to the organization."

"I knew it!" Amy crowed. "You *are* working for the organization!" She allowed herself a brief moment of triumph and was about to say "I told you so" to her mother when she remembered her precarious situation. She was in no position to feel triumphant.

"And what does the organization plan to do with the gene?" Nancy demanded. "Destroy half the world's population? Or *all* of it?"

"Not at all," Devon said. "There are no plans for mass destruction. The organization will simply study the gene."

"For what purpose?" Dr. Dave asked.

Amy thought she knew. "Genetic experiments, I bet."

"Yes," said Devon. "We can use it to create a genetic antibody. The Plague is the most potent genetic disease that has ever evolved. It can be manipulated and treated and combined to produce a protection against all disorders. Engineering this one gene can take the place of a total genetic overhaul."

"Are you saying you want to use this gene to make humans stronger?" Dr. Dave asked in disbelief.

The clone corrected him. "*Some* humans. Those whose bodies can deal with the side effects."

"What about the others?" Nancy asked.

"It will kill them," Devon said. "This one gene has the potential to eliminate the weakest in the human population. Quickly and neatly, and without taking the time to study every different genetic structure. The organization will be able to reach its goals more quickly. We will create a perfect human species."

"I thought that was what you wanted the Amys and Andys to do," Nancy said.

Amy understood. "They don't want to wait for us to

grow up and mate and produce genetically superior people. They're not very patient people."

"Precisely," Devon said. "The organization has been unable to replicate Project Crescent. The destruction of the laboratory fourteen years ago resulted in the loss of highly significant data and set the entire plan back."

"That was the intention," Nancy said coldly.

Devon continued. "Of course, the Project Crescent clones can be used to achieve the goals through natural evolution. We have attempted to accelerate their growth so that they could begin the process sooner. In fact, this Amy, Number Seven, was the test for this plan. She was implanted with a timing device for genetic acceleration."

Amy remembered waking up on her thirteenth birthday to find that she had aged about ten years. Now she understood why none of the other Amys or Andys had had the same experience.

Dr. Dave was gazing at Devon intently. "But even if you can accelerate the growth of these clones, there are not enough of them to develop the kind of population you want."

"Not true," Devon said. "Ultimately, our goal could be achieved. But it could take a thousand years. With the Plague gene, a population of perfect humans can be developed in less than one full generation." He spoke matter-of-factly, without any emotion.

Amy watched in alarm as an unfamiliar expression came over her mother's face. A look of resignation. Nancy took a test tube out of the rack next to Tasha's gurney. "And if we don't give you this gene . . ."

"Then we take Number Seven. It is possible that a complete dissection will replace some of the information that was lost in the laboratory explosion."

Nancy studied the test tube. "How strange," she said, "to think that the contents of this tiny tube can change the world."

"Don't give it to him, Mom! Let him take me! I'll get away."

Nancy looked at her sadly. "I can't risk that, darling."

Amy was horrified. With the transfer of that little glass tube, the entire world would change. She made one more attempt to free herself. She opened her mouth and clamped on to one of the hands that were holding her. With all her might, with every bit of strength she could muster, she bit into the flesh.

She thought the pain or the shock would force Devon to loosen his grip. But she felt no release. What was even more curious was the fact that he didn't react at all—not even with a cry of pain.

This didn't make sense. From experience, she knew

that engineered clones could withstand a lot of pain. But they were not impervious to it. He had to have felt *something*.

She realized that her mother and the doctor were staring at the hand she'd bitten. She took a good look, and gasped.

She expected to see blood, maybe some exposed bone. But only wires protruded from the hole in the wrist. He wasn't a clone at all.

"Let her go," Nancy said grimly. She extended the test tube toward him. The android-robot—whatever it was—took the tube in his good hand and released Amy from the damaged hand.

"Thank you," the Devon-bot said politely. And he walked out of the room.

Amy watched as the door swung shut. It was like a door closing on life itself. This was it. The organization would use that gene to take over the world.

She couldn't stop the tears. After all she'd just been through . . . after all the confrontations, the close calls, the escapes she'd managed over the years . . . the organization was going to win.

She threw herself into her mother's arms and wept. Nancy stroked her hair. "It's all right, Amy. Really, everything's going to be fine."

Amy looked up. "Mom, how can you say that?" Her

vision was blurred by the tears. But she could still see that her mother was smiling. *Smiling!*

And so was Dr. Dave. He'd taken another test tube from the rack. "*This* is the Plague gene, Amy. When we extracted you from Tasha's genome, your mother separated you from the genetic material. While Devon was busy seeing if you had come back undamaged, she also separated the Plague gene from the rest."

"I could tell that the other genes were nonfunctioning," Nancy said. "They won't provide Devon or the organization with any new information."

Dr. Dave was already sitting at the desk, studying a smear of the Plague gene under a microscope. "I can get the antidote made up right now," he said. "It will be shipped by air to every clinic and hospital in the world. By this time tomorrow, every victim of the Plague will be on the road to recovery."

"And we'll be able to make a vaccine," Nancy added. "So no one will ever suffer from this disease again."

Amy's tears had dried. "Mom, you're brilliant! You too, Dr. Dave," she added hastily.

"I just wish I could see the faces of those organization guys when they examine what they got under a microscope," he said with satisfaction.

Nancy laughed. "Can you imagine their disappointment? They'll think they have the means to take over the world when all they've got is a mess of worthless leftover genetic material."

Amy too had to smile at the thought of how the organization would react. But she was thinking about something else too. Her squatters . . .

Nancy Candler was wrong. They weren't worthless.

f i f t e e n

Tasha's face was still pale, but her eyes were bright. And a little disappointed.

"You *talked* to the fat gene? And you couldn't convince it to get repaired?"

"It didn't *need* repair, Tasha," Amy explained patiently. "There's nothing wrong with it. That gene is part of what makes you *you*."

"I could be a thinner me," Tasha said mournfully.

"Oh, shut up," Eric said with a grin. "You're alive. Isn't that enough?"

Tasha had to smile back. "Yeah. It's pretty good." She

turned to Amy. "I still can't believe you were inside my genome! What did it look like?"

"Like any old genome," Amy said airily. "If you've seen one, you've seen them all."

Tasha laughed. Her eyes were soft as she gazed at Amy. "Thank you," she said. "You saved my life."

"She saved the *world*," Eric corrected. "No more Plague. Amy, you're amazing."

Amy didn't argue. This was no time for modesty. "Thank you."

"Of course," Eric continued, "it's really your mother who deserves the thanks. She was the one who tricked that Devon robot into taking the worthless genes."

Amy glared at him in mock exasperation. "But if it wasn't for me, she wouldn't have had any worthless genes to give him. And they weren't worthless. Those squatters gave their lives for Tasha."

"I wish I could thank them," Tasha said. Her voice was becoming drowsy.

"You need to rest," Amy told her. But Tasha didn't need the advice. She was already asleep. Amy and Eric tiptoed out of the hospital room.

"The doctor says she can leave tomorrow," Eric told her. "She'll have to stay home for a week, and by then she's supposed to be back to normal."

"That's good news," Amy said.

"No kidding," Eric noted. "I won't have to be so nice to her anymore."

Amy laughed, but she gave Eric a reproving look at the same time. "I just hope this has taught you to appreciate your sister."

"Yeah, I do feel different," Eric admitted. After a second, he added, "Not just about her."

Amy wasn't quite sure what he meant, but she had her suspicions. She smiled and waited to see if she was right.

Eric had a hard time meeting her eyes. "You know, I didn't mean that, about just your mother deserving thanks for saving Tasha. I was just teasing. You're the real hero. Thank you."

"You're welcome," Amy said. After a second, she said, "But that's not the only thing you've kidded me about recently."

"What do you mean?"

"Just before I went into the capsule to be reduced, you said something. . . ." She couldn't bring herself to actually use the words. It would embarrass him to be reminded that he had said, "I love you."

Eric flushed. "Oh yeah. I remember." He was silent for a moment. "Amy?"

"What?"

His eyes met hers. "I wasn't kidding."

Memo from the Director

We regret to announce that the organization has failed to obtain the Plague gene. Thus, we have decided to reinstate the original plan. A master race will be created from the Project Crescent clones. The organization is aware that previous attempts to put this plan into motion have failed. Due to the difficulties of trapping the subjects, a new means of putting the clones into service has been drafted.

The organization will no longer attempt to kidnap or lure the clones. The clones will come to the organization—voluntarily, willingly, and ready to join in our mission.

Don't miss

replica

Fast Forward

The Plague Trilogy
Book III

BREAKING NEWS! There's a genetic freak among us!
Being perfect isn't a big deal to Amy—until word
gets out that she's a clone. Now everyone is shunning
her, and she's getting mad. She starts to believe that the
organization has the right idea: The world would be a
better place if only Project Crescent clones existed.

With a little help, Amy gets what she wishes for. She
enters a world where everyone is just like her. But even
perfection has its flaws. . . .